"When I first went to live with the Smith Sound Eskimos, it was not long before I became acquainted with the strange songs and fabulous legends relating the greatness of a man the natives called 'Mahri Pahluk.' I had followed Peary's North Pole expedition into that country by a year and so I soon realized that the man around whom these stories had grown was Matthew Henson."

—Peter Freuchen, 1928

The following story is a fictionalized account of the life of Matthew Henson. Events and quotes have been combined or condensed for dramatic effect.

Story and art by Simon Schwartz
Translation by Laura Watkinson

First American edition published in 2015 by Graphic Universe™.
Published by arrangement with Avant-Verlag.

Packeis by Simon Schwartz
Copyright © Simon Schwartz & Avant-Verlag 2012. Rights arranged through Nicolas Grivel Agency.

English translation copyright © 2015 by Laura Watkinson

Graphic Universe™ is a trademark of Lerner Publishing Group, Inc.

Graphic Universe™
A division of Lerner Publishing Group, Inc.
241 First Avenue North
Minneapolis, MN 55401 USA

For reading levels and more information, look up this title at www.lernerbooks.com.

The photographs in this book are used with the permission of: Library of Congress, pp. 155–158. Map on p. 154 © Laura Westlund/Independent Picture Service.

Primary dialogue font created by Simon Schwartz.

The Cataloging-in-Publication Data for *First Man: Reimagining Matthew Henson* is on file at the Library of Congress.
ISBN 978-1-4677-5842-0 (lb : alk. paper)
ISBN 978-1-4677-8106-0 (pb : alk. paper)
ISBN 978-1-4677-8856-4 (eb pdf)

Manufactured in the United States of America
1 – DP – 7/15/15

First MAN

Simon Schwartz

Reimagining
MATTHEW HENSON

Translated by Laura Watkinson

Graphic Universe™ • Minneapolis

Introduction

A few years ago, a German weekly newspaper contacted me to commission illustrations for an article on polar expeditions. Of course, Robert Peary was a part of the article. I bought several books to learn more about the official discoverer of the North Pole, and in one of those books, I came across a little blurry photo of a man of color. Underneath the picture—in a tone that seemed to romanticize the racial imbalance—was a caption that read, "Robert Peary's faithful black servant, Matthew Henson." Who was this man? I had never heard of Matthew Henson, and the book included no further information. My detective instincts kicked in!

When I found out a little later that Henson had reached the North Pole before Peary, I was stunned. This historical injustice, Henson's lack of recognition, made me angry. At the same time, I was full of admiration and respect for Henson's work, selflessness, and humility.

As I began my search for more information, I was shocked by how little had been published about Matthew Henson. In recent years, the body of literature has grown considerably, but not sufficiently. Full of enthusiasm, I tracked down Matthew Henson's own accounts of his life and travels in an antique shop. After that, I knew many facts but still shockingly little about the man himself. What did he believe himself to stand for? What did he think about the everyday racism in his life? Despite the information I now had about Henson, his personality remained as far away as the North Pole.

The reason behind my decision to draw this book, however, was learning that Matthew Henson has become part of Inuit mythology as the mystical figure Mahri Pahluk. I realized that there was even more to Henson's life than the discovery of the North Pole. Beyond the social significance of Henson's travels, his life story contains a lesson about how we remember our history.

Western culture seems to be based in an objective view of history and the world in which we live. "On April 6, 1909, Robert Peary discovered the North Pole." This sounds like a fact, but the person who put it forward is Peary himself. Should we not begin to doubt? Peary actually began work on his own legend before he even left Greenland. He borrowed his personal credo from Hannibal, the famed general of antiquity: "I shall find a way or make one."

Some indigenous cultures remember their history more subjectively—through myths, legends, and songs. Anyone within these cultures can retell a shared history, adapting it to his or her own life experiences or that of his or her listeners. I will not say that this kind of historiography is better, but it seems to me much more honest and open, because a good view of history is a collection of many subjective memories. And the legends of the Inuit do justice to Matthew Henson—to Mahri Pahluk—by presenting him as a kind of early superhero. (So my reference to another comic book hero at the end of the book was not done without reason.)

I am not a historian but a graphic novelist, which is why I made no attempt at nonfiction. I played with the story. I tried to tell a fictionalized version of Matthew Henson's life based on facts. I gave myself freedom with the narrative, although readers can find a timeline at the back of the book that doesn't take the same liberties.

Some sections, such as Captain Childs's advice to a young Matthew Henson, I took from Henson's own writings. Another important inspiration was an old newspaper article that briefly described Henson's wife Lucy—an agile and confident woman. She was a kind of counterpoint to her almost stubbornly quiet husband. Through Lucy, I could ask a lot of questions about Henson that may strike modern readers. But I would have been a hypocrite if I had tried to present the answers to these questions in my book. Henson is silent.

To the end, Henson has been a hard subject to get a hold on. Again and again, he seems to me almost like a phantom. Sometimes I can see him through a passing snowstorm, but then he disappears again. We should look for him together and remember his great achievements—each of us in our own subjective way.

Simon Schwartz, Hamburg 2015

High in the North, in the coldest spot on Earth, lives Tahnusuk.

The Devil.

For when the Raven created the world, he banished the Devil to that place so Tahnusuk could do the people no harm.

The Raven took good care of the people. He showed them how to hunt, how to make clothes, and how to build houses.

And because the great bird was so powerful and so benevolent, he blessed them with three sacred stones.

The stones gave the people weapons for hunting and fishing, so the people kept the stones well hidden from the devil Tahnusuk.

The people led a happy life until the Oopernadeet—the visitors who come in spring—landed on their coast.

They were ruthless and obsessed with finding Tahnusuk.

And among those same Oopernadeet, there was also Mahri Pahluk.

13

14

The wise old captain took great care of Mahri Pahluk, just as the Raven cares for his people. Together they traveled all over the world, seeing strange and mysterious places, and Mahri Pahluk learned about the important things in life.

It was a happy time, and they were like father and son.

But nobody lives forever. One day the sea goddess Sedna, a daughter of the devil Tahnusuk, took the old man, leaving Mahri Pahluk all alone.

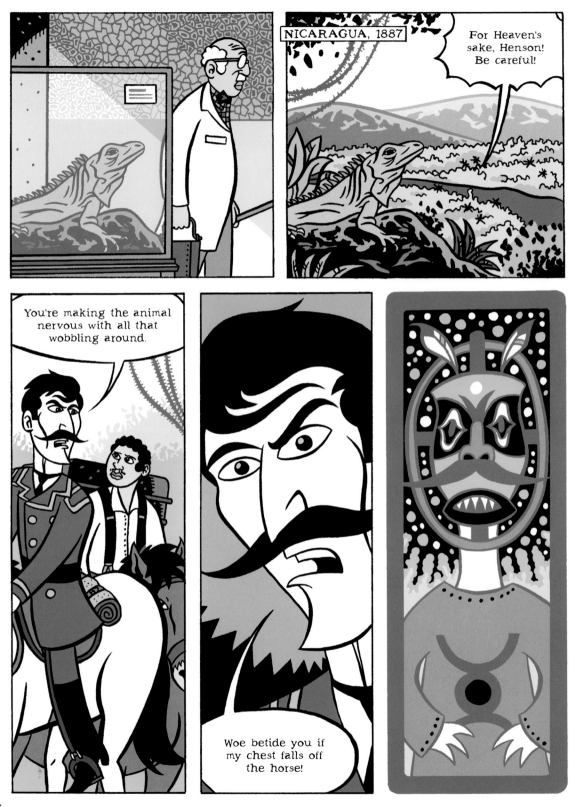

May I help you?

In the expanses of the polar ice, Doctor, there are still things for a man to discover. Here, there's nothing but mosquitoes.

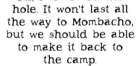

Sir, I've sealed the hole. It won't last all the way to Mombacho, but we should be able to make it back to the camp.

I doubt that, Matt. He's not fond of the climate here.

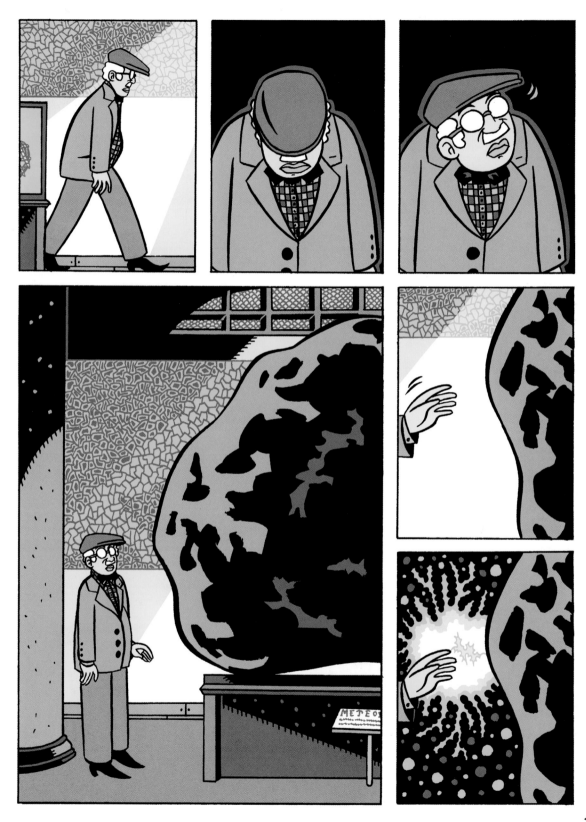

Only a proud and God-fearing nation such as ours is worthy of conquering the North Pole. And when I have succeeded in achieving this goal, there will be hardly an American who does not feel a little better, a little prouder to be a citizen of these United States.

... my beloved wife, Josephine, whose feminine charms will bring a touch of warmth and coziness to the icy Arctic.

DAVIS STRAIT, 1891

Where are we now approximately, Captain Bartlett?

Near the sixty-fifth degree of latitude, Dr. Cook.

We've left the Labrador Sea and are heading for Baffin Bay. Once we're past the bay, we'll be almost at our destination in Greenland.

And you, boy—better take care you don't freeze to death. After all, you don't really belong in this climate, do you?

Captain Bartlett, please! Mr. Henson's ethnological background says absolutely nothing about his ability to survive the cold!

Hey, I just wanted to warn him.

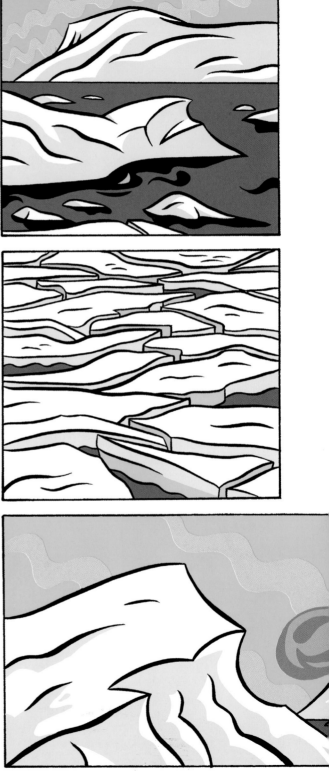

ETAH, 1892

Hey Matt! Could you please come down from the roof and go get your camera?

I'd like you to take a farewell photo of me, Qisuk, and little Minik before I leave for the Pole with the commander and Captain Bartlett.

Disappointed, the Oopernadeet returned from their expedition. They had not reached their goal and had been forced to turn back. Mahri Pahluk tried to tell them what had happened to him, but they didn't listen. And on their journey home, the devil Tahnusuk drove the first wedge into the group.

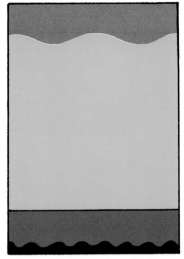

Ladies and gentlemen, in a few minutes we'll be arriving in Dawson, Georgia.

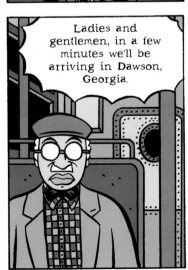

73

Commander?

Commander, can you hear me?

You saved my life, Doctor.

No, no. All you have to thank me for is the bandage. Matt heard you calling, dug you out, and carried you almost the entire way back to Etah.

Oh, how can I ever thank you, Henson? And I once thought you were barely good enough to wash my shirts. I'd be dead without you.

But what is my wretched life worth? I'll never have the satisfaction of reaching the Pole.

Why do you say that? We'll just give it another try.

And while the Oopernadeet dragged away the three sacred stones, the Raven cast out the shaman for his betrayal and gave him to the devil Tahnusuk.

You cannot be serious! This is human trafficking!

The savages will be an asset to the Museum of Natural History.

But if you are frightened of scientific progress, Dr. Cook, I no longer have any need for your services!

You're going to regret this, Peary! Bitterly!

?

For a sailor you sure have a weak stomach. Ha ha!

86

Ah, there you are. Where were you all day?

I haven't gotten around to doing any housework today. My friend Mavis lent me this new novel...

...about a young man who travels from England to Transylvania, because there's this count who wants to buy a house in London. But the count turns out to be a vampire...

...and, oh my, it's so exciting... The part I'm reading now... the count's just drinking the blood of a beautiful woman...

...and the creepiest thing is that she's called Lucy, like me, and the count sleeps in a coffin and...

When Mahri Pahluk and the other Oopernadeet returned, the people lived in fear of them.

The breath of Tahnusuk clung to the visitors.

Only those people who had given up faith in themselves joined the Oopernadeet in their new search.

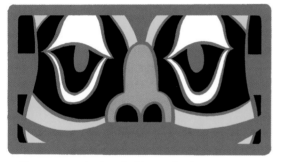

The Oopernadeet called Peary had come up with a new plan. As they made their way across the ice, he sent men back to the camp, using their strength at first and then discarding their weight.

But the devil Tahnusuk steered Peary's decisions, and so some brave men did not find their way back.

Finally, only Peary, Mahri Pahluk, the Oopernadeet Bartlett, and six others remained.

Bartlett, you'll return tomorrow with two natives.

What? You can't be serious!

I have made my decision.

Do you intend to take Henson with you? He has no understanding of navigation!

98

Good. Now that Captain Bartlett has left us, we will embark upon the last leg of our journey, Matt.

According to my measurements, we are no more than 35 miles from our goal.

You'll go ahead with two savages and create a navigable channel. Then I'll follow you.

At your command, sir.

CRAAAACK!

Well, just over a week ago, your former colleague Dr. Cook arrived here with two savages, half-starved to death. He claims to have reached the North Pole a year ago.

On the way back, he was forced to spend the winter in the ice. Which is why he's only just found his way back to civilization to announce his triumph.

He left a chest full of his instruments and diaries with me. You only just missed him, Commander.

Mr. Henson.

Take this chest and dispose of it in the sea.

What? Are you insane? Just because Cook discovered the Pole before you? I will not permit this! This chest is staying with me!

You still need someone to take you back to your beloved red deer, don't you?

NEW YORK, SEPTEMBER 16, 1909

Matt!

COOK HAS GOOD WORDS FOR PEARY

The First American to Reach the Pole Praises His Rival.

Says He Hopes the Report of Peary's Success Is True.

Declares the Observations and Reports of Peary Will Confirm His.

The North Pole, Cook Says, Is Big Enough for Two.

Peary Expresses Doubt About Cook Finding The North Pole

The Drifting Ice,

SCIE

POPULA

ol. CI. - No. 12.
ESTABLISHED 1845.

NEW ORL

NANSEN
1895

FRANZ JOSEPH LAND

CAGNI
1900

SPITZBERGEN

NORTH POLE

COMITURE 120.

87° 6'

PEARY
1906

GREENLAND SEA

60°

Petit Journal

SUPPLÉMENT ILLUSTRÉ

5 CENT.   5 CENT.

Nombre pür

X.me Année
DIMANCHE 19 SEPTEMBRE 1909

PÔLE NORD

DR. FREDERICK A. COOK LECTURES

In which the Arctic explorer tells graphically of his thrilling Arctic experiences; answers, *in toto* for the first time, the pro-Peary charges against him, and exposes, by sensational evidence, bribery and fraud in the campaign to discredit him.

The charges made against Dr. Cook were not so amazing as Dr. Cook's own exposé of his defamers. The most gripping, thrilling narrative of human hardship ever told.

Illustrated by marvelous, colored pictures.

CONQUEST OF THE POLE.
—The Discovery of New Worlds of Crystal Glory.
ER LECTURES BY DR. COOK:
tarctic—A Comparative View of the Two Poles.
e—Explorations in the Antarctic and an Account of
Earth's Southern Apex.
he Ascent of Mt. McKinley.

was the climacteric hour of my life. The vision and the thrill,
ins, and will remain with me as long as life lasts, as the
accomplishment. . . .
ny enemies were watched, and I am here now to uncover
cy ever forged in a strife for honor. . . .
which the North Pole and any honor accruing to its dis-
a spirit which was almost broken, of a man whose
hands."—Dr. Cook.

1-1912 are now being booked. During
es at the Chautauqua assemblages
e confirmed by

rbrid

BO
HRO

rades an

n Addres
Fa

Morrison Out
Ped

118

Picayune.

NS. LA., TUESDAY, SEPTEMBER 7, 1909.

NO

ANOTHER AMERICAN EXPLORER REACHED THE NORTH PO

Commander Robert E. Peary Reports That His Expedition Was Crowned With Success.

The Explorer Cables That He "Nailed the Stars and Stripes the North Pole" April 6, 1909—The Message Flashed From Indian Harbor, Labrador.

PEARY CABLES HIS WIFE OF HIS

South Harpswell, Me., Sept. 6.—Command nounced his success in discovering the N summering here at Eagle Island

"Indian Harbor, via Ca

"Mrs. R. E. P

"Have ma

Will

COOK'S PLAN THRILL

Offer to Send Back for E Stirs Interest of Partisans.

[BY DIRECT WIRE TO THE T
COPENHAGEN, Sept.
[Exclusive Dispatch.] Cope
hagen interest in the Coo
Peary pole controversy grew in
tense today, when it became
known that Dr Cook announced
he would charter a steamer at
his own expense and send it to
Greenland for the Eskimos who
accompanied him on his polar
dash, and have them corrobo-
rate his story. The steamer
probably will be under command of Capt. Sverdrup, the
Norwegian Arctic explorer. It
is said that J. Pierpont Mor-
gan telegraphed to Dr Cook
offering him any sum he might
need, but the explorer says he
will pay for the expedition
herself.

The Danish interpreter in
North Greenland says that
Commander Peary's allegations
were absurd to those who know
the facts. According to this au-
thority Dr Cook was not
led to escape observation i.e.
which was impossible in any
event, but in pursuance of a
plan based on Peary's own ex-
perience with the easterly drift
of ice in the polar sea north of
Greenland.

In Two Parts Complete—28 Pages.

The LOS ANGELES

SEPTEMBER 10, 1909.

Twenty-Eighth Year.

PER ANNUM $9.00 { Per Month, 75 Cents, or 2½ Cents a Copy.

THE WEATHER.
BRIEF REPORT.

FORECAST—For Los Angeles and vicinity: Fair; overcast in morning; light north wind. For San Francisco and vicinity: Fair; light west winds, increasing.
Sunrise, 5:33; sunset, 6:07; moon rises 2:36 a.m. Saturday.
YESTERDAY—Maximum tempera-ture, 77 deg.; minimum 56 deg.
Wind, 5 a.m., southwest; velocity 3 miles; 5 p.m. southwest; velocity 7 miles. At midnight the temperature was 59 deg.; clear.
TODAY—At 2 a.m. the temperature was 57 deg.; clear.
[The comparative weather report, in-cluding comparative temperatures, will be found on page 12, Part II.]

The Times

THRILLING ACCOUNT

ICE AND VIOLENT WINDS GIVE PEARY HARD FIGH

*Noted Explorer Tells of Desperate Strugg
Start of Polar Expedition.*

*Remarkable Narrative of Trip to North Pole by
Naval Officer, Greatest Arctic Traveler of the
Thrilling Tale of Discovery.*

Well, it's not that hard. You can start by carrying these crates into the next hall.

You'll get ten cents a day. I'll be back in an hour. Got it, boy?

I have grave doubts about Dr. Cook's supposed discovery of the North Pole. If he had truly dared to walk to the Pole, he would have starved to death, given the equipment he claims to have taken. Besides, he has still not published his diaries for the world to see.

I have known him for years as a dubious and unscrupulous individual. I distrust not only his fairy tales about the Pole but also his supposed ascent of Mount McKinley.

Yes, sir.

It saddens me to hear such accusations from a Navy man. Of course I climbed to the summit of Mount McKinley with my partner Ed Barrill. The facts are indisputable.

As far as my diaries are concerned, they were destroyed on the instructions of Commander Peary after I entrusted them to my friend Harry Whitney.

A civilian like Dr. Cook should be ashamed to speak about a member of the US Navy in such terms. My assistant Matthew Henson, who speaks the savages' language fluently, questioned Dr. Cook's native companions on my behalf.

They indicated that they remained on land the entire time, never traveling by water. To be honest, I do not believe that the group ever left Greenland.

I consider most untrustworthy a man who would send back an asset such as Captain Bartlett shortly before the goal, who did not make a note in his diary on the day of his so-called triumph, and who would pay heed to the ridiculous prattling of a nigger!

Excuse me. Are you Matthew Henson?

But Matt, some things will never change.

Mahri Pahluk was the greatest and most heroic man who had ever lived, the equal of the gods . . .

. . . but the devil Tahnusuk mocked Mahri Pahluk.

141

Sorry to bother you, Mr. Henson.

Yes?

Could I ask you to use the gentlemen's bathroom in the basement?

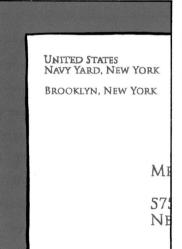

UNITED STATES
NAVY YARD, NEW YORK

BROOKLYN, NEW YORK

ME

57
NE

147

ETAH, 1962

Show me too!

No! It's not for girls.

No way! Superman is for girls too!

Heh.

Look at him flying through the sky!

And there! He's stopping the comet!

Superman's the greatest. He's like a god.

What's this nonsense you're talking?

The End

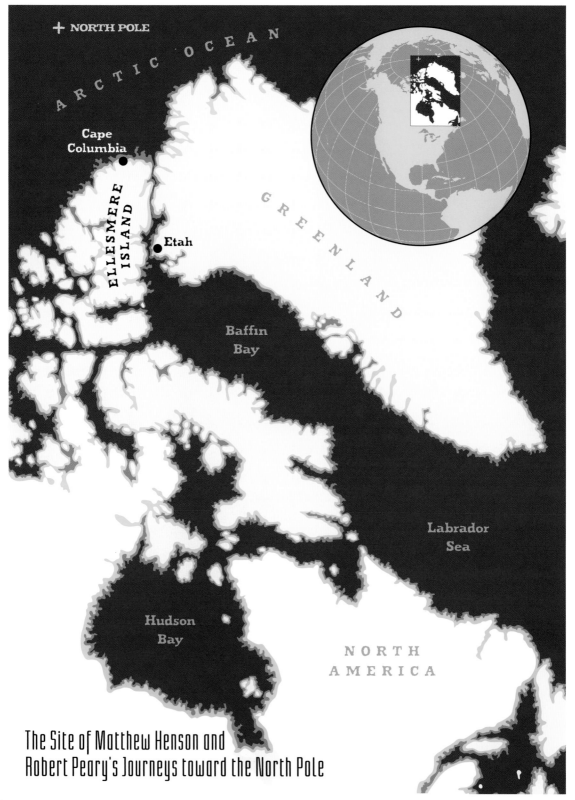

+ NORTH POLE

ARCTIC OCEAN

Cape
Columbia

ELLESMERE ISLAND

Etah

GREENLAND

Baffin
Bay

Labrador
Sea

Hudson
Bay

NORTH
AMERICA

The Site of Matthew Henson and
Robert Peary's Journeys toward the North Pole

Chronology

First Man: Reimagining Matthew Henson is a literary retelling of Matthew Henson's life. Not all aspects of the graphic account are historically accurate. The list below presents milestones from the life of Matthew Henson in chronological order.

August 8, 1866: Matthew Alexander Henson is born in Charles County, Maryland. His parents die shortly after that, and he grows up with his Aunt Janey in Washington, DC.

1879: At the age of twelve, Matthew Henson makes his way to Baltimore. He joins the crew of the *Katie Hines* under Captain Childs. His travels take him to Asia, Africa, Europe, and elsewhere.

1883: On a return journey from Jamaica, Captain Childs dies at sea after a serious illness. Matthew Henson leaves the seafaring life.

1887: Robert Peary meets Matthew Henson at the hat store B.J. Steinmetz & Sons in Washington, DC. Peary employs Henson as a valet on the store owner's recommendation. In Nicaragua, Peary gives Henson surveying tasks to perform.

1888: Peary and Henson return to the United States, where Peary gets Henson a job at a navy yard.

April 16, 1891: Henson marries twenty-two-year-old Eva Helen Flint in Philadelphia.

1891-1892: Peary takes a crew to Greenland with the aim of exploring the unknown north coast. He takes Henson along as an unpaid volunteer. Dr. Fredrick Cook accompanies this team but leaves after a fight with Peary. Henson soon learns the language of the Inuit and wins their trust. They call him *Mahri Pahluk*—"Matthew, the kind one." Henson teaches Inuit survival strategies to Peary and the other team members.

1893: After a grueling lecture tour and attempts to curry favor with influential personalities, Peary sets off for Greenland a third time. Matthew Henson is once again part of the team.

1894: As injury and bad weather threaten the expedition, Peary sends his wife and a large part of the crew back to the United States. Only Henson and journalist Hugh Lee remain with him.

1895: Henson, Peary, Lee, and six Inuit make an attempt on the Pole. Storms and a lack of food force the team to abandon the attempt. Henson saves Peary's life when a musk ox attacks him, and Inuit later rescue the starving team. Following the attempt on the Pole, Peary insists on sailing down the coast of Greenland to transport two massive meteorites that are sacred to the Inuit.

Matthew Henson, 1910

1896: The transportation of a third meteorite takes almost a year. Josephine Peary sells the meteorites to the American Museum of Natural History for $40,000, and Henson is given a post at the museum as a taxidermist.

1897: Henson and his wife Eva divorce. Robert Peary gives six living Inuit to the American Museum of Natural History for the purposes of anthropological research, including Qisuk and his ten-year-old son, Minik. All of them except for the child die of tuberculosis within a short time. Minik is taken in by a senior member of the museum staff. His father's skeleton is preserved and exhibited at the museum.

1898: Peary sets off for the North Pole again, this time just with Henson and the doctor T.S. Dedrick Jr. Once again, bad weather hampers the mission. Peary loses eight toes.

1902: After four years and many attempts to conquer the North Pole, Henson, Peary, and T.S. Dedrick Jr. return to the United States. Henson starts work as a railway porter.

1905: At a dinner in his honor, Henson meets the young Lucy Ross. Peary and Henson set off again for the Pole, this time under the command of Captain Robert Bartlett. The ship comes within around 500 miles (805 kilometers) of the Pole. During this expedition, an Inuit woman, Akatingwah, gives birth to Henson's son, Anauakaq.

April 21, 1906: Henson and Peary make an advance on the North Pole. The attempt fails, but the two men come closer to the Pole than any person before.

September 1907: After Henson returns to the United States, he and Lucy Ross marry in New York.

July 8, 1908: Henson, Peary, Bartlett, and other members of an expedition team leave New York on the *Roosevelt*.

1909: Henson, Peary, and the team leave Cape Columbia in February and set off on a walk of around 410 miles (660 km) to the Pole. As they travel closer to the Pole, Peary sends team members back to the base. This allows him to take advantage of their strength during the early stages while later saving their transport weight.

Men and sled dogs use a piece of iceberg to cross a stream at the North Pole, circa 1909.

From left: Donald Baxter MacMillan, George Borup, Robert Bartlett, and Matthew Henson sit on the sledge that went to the North Pole, circa 1909.

March 26, 1909: The team breaks Peary's 1906 record.

April 1, 1909: Peary makes the controversial decision to send back Bartlett, a respected navigator, around 149 miles (240 km) from the North Pole. Bartlett protests, but Peary gives preference to Henson.

April 5, 1909: On the basis of his own measurements, Peary estimates the distance to the North Pole to be only another 40 miles (64 km).

April 6, 1909: In two teams with two Inuit each, Peary and Henson begin their walk to the North Pole. Just a few miles from their goal, Henson falls through thin ice and into the freezing water below, but the Inuit Ootah rescues him. After about four hours, Henson estimates that they have arrived. Peary, who arrives later, confirms with his measurements that they have reached their goal. Peary later raises a US flag

and takes a few blurred photographs, which cannot be used to confirm his measurements. According to Henson, the greatly debilitated Peary has a fit of depression on the return journey. Henson is forced to take charge and get the team home.

September 1, 1909: Frederick Cook announces by telegram that he discovered the North Pole on April 21, 1908.

September 6, 1909: Peary sends a telegram to announce his own discovery of the North Pole on April 6, 1909.

September 16, 1909: Matthew Henson lands in New York.

November 1909: The National Geographic Society declares Robert Peary the sole discoverer of the North Pole, following a public feud between Peary and Cook. The society also awards a medal to Captain Bartlett while ignoring Matthew Henson's achievement.

1910: Matthew Henson starts work at a parking garage in Brooklyn, New York. However, the theater producer and boxing promoter William Aloysius Brady persuades him to go on lecture tours. Henson's poor health and Robert Peary's lawyers hamper these tours. In the Arctic, Danish explorer Peter Freuchen hears Inuit legends and songs about a mythical being called Mahri Pahluk. Freuchen realizes that this is Matthew Henson, whom he does not meet in person until many years later in the United States.

1912: *A Negro Explorer at the North Pole*, Henson's account of his travels, is published with a foreword by Robert Peary. Peary has otherwise ended all contact with Henson, not responding to his letters and requests for money.

1913: Henson is appointed as a clerk at the US Customs House in New York.

February 19, 1920: Peary falls into a coma as a result of pernicious anemia and dies the following day in Washington, D.C. He is buried with full military honors at Arlington National Cemetery. Some experts still doubt Peary's claims to have discovered the North Pole.

1937: After almost thirty years as a clerk at the US Customs House, Henson retires at the age of seventy.

1944: The United States Congress awards Henson a version of the medal of honor that was given to Robert Peary more than thirty years earlier.

1947: Henson and cowriter Bradley Robinson publish *Dark Companion*, Henson's novelized autobiography. That same year sees the publication of the first issue of the comic book *Negro Heroes*, which contains what is likely the first comic about Matthew Henson.

April 6, 1954: President Dwight D. Eisenhower invites Henson and his wife Lucy to the White House.

March 9, 1955: Henson dies in New York and is buried at Woodlawn Cemetery in the Bronx.

1968: Lucy Henson dies in New York and is buried beside her husband at Woodlawn Cemetery.

1988: Matthew Henson and Lucy Henson are reburied at Arlington National Cemetery.

1993: The bones of the Inuit who died after Peary and Henson brought them to New York are returned to their homeland for burial.

2000: The National Geographic Society posthumously awards the prestigious Hubbard Medal—for distinction in exploration, discovery, and research—to Matthew Henson.

Matthew Henson holding a portrait of Robert E. Peary, 1953

Selected Bibliography

Burton, Rosemary, Richard Cavendish, and Bernard Stonehouse. *Journeys of the Great Explorers*. New York: Facts on File, 1992.

Henson, Matthew Alexander. *A Negro Explorer at the North Pole*. New York: Arno Press, 1969.

Johnson, Dolores. *Onward: A Photobiography of African-American Polar Explorer Matthew Henson*. Washington, DC: National Geographic, 2006.

Peary, Robert E. *The North Pole: Its Discovery in 1909 under the Auspices of the Peary Arctic Club*. New York: Dover Publications, 1986.

Robinson, Bradley. *Dark Companion*. New York: R. M. McBride, 1947.

"Veteran Explorer Finds Radio Enlivens Adventure: Looking Back Across the Ice." *New York Times*, April 17, 1932. Accessed January 7, 2015. http://matthewhenson.com/1932_NY_times/henson_NYT_radio1932.pdf.

About the Author

Simon Schwartz was born in Erfurt in 1982 and grew up in the Kreuzberg neighborhood of Berlin. In 2004, he relocated to Hamburg to study illustration at the Hamburg University of Applied Sciences. Five years later, he had completed his debut graphic novel, *drüben!*, now available in the United States as *The Other Side of the Wall*. In 2010, the book won the ICOM Independent Comic Prize in the Outstanding Scenario category and was nominated for the German Youth Literature Prize. In 2012, his second graphic novel, *Packeis*, won the Max-und-Moritz Prize for Best German Comic. *Packeis* is now available in the United States as *First Man: Reimagining Matthew Henson*.

Simon Schwartz's comics and illustrations are published regularly in various newspapers and magazines, including *Frankfurter Allgemeine Sonntagszeitung, Der Freitag, GEOlino* and *Die Zeit*. He currently teaches illustration at the Hamburg University of Applied Sciences. More of his work is viewable online at www.simon-schwartz.com.